A JIGSAW JONES MYSTERY®

The Case of the Groaning Ghost

by James Preller
illustrated by Jamie Smith
cover illustration by R. W. Alley

A
LITTLE APPLE
PAPERBACK

SCHOLASTIC INC.
New York   Toronto   London   Auckland   Sydney
Mexico City   New Delhi   Hong Kong   Buenos Aires

Read all the Jigsaw Jones Mysteries!

*For Craig Walker, who can make
any problem go away.*

ISBN-13: 978-0-439-89624-5
ISBN-10: 0-439-89624-X

Text copyright © 2006 by James Preller.
Illustrations copyright © 2006 by Scholastic Inc.

12 11 10 9 8 7 6 5 4 3 2   6 7 8 9 10 11/0

Special thanks to Robin Wasserman

Printed in the U.S.A.
First printing, October 2006

Contents

Chapter One

The Disappearing Client

"We've got trouble," I said into the phone. "Trouble with a capital *T*."

"Oh, yeah?" Mila Yeh replied. "What kind of trouble?"

"Here's a clue," I said. "It rhymes with *Solofsky*."

Mila chuckled. "I'll be right over," she said, and hung up the phone.

Ever since kindergarten, Bobby Solofsky has been a stone in my shoe. A lump in my pillow. A worm in my apple. A fly in my grape juice. A . . .

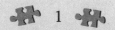

Well, you get the idea.

Why is Solofsky such a pain in my side? I wouldn't know where to start. But if I did, it might be here:

Reason 1. Everyone in the world calls me Jigsaw. Why? Solving puzzles is my game, so Jigsaw's my name. Only two people call me by my real name, Theodore. The first one is my mom. That's okay, because she's the one who gave it to me. And the second one? You guessed it. Solofsky.

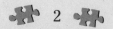

But that's not the only reason. There's also:

2. Solofsky makes gross sucking sounds with his teeth and chews tuna fish sandwiches with his mouth open.

3. He's the kind of guy who would steal candy from a baby. (I'm not kidding. I've seen him do it.)

4. He tortures bugs.

5. Did I mention he calls me Theodore?

Now I had something new to add to the list. Thanks to Solofsky, five of my best friends had just disappeared. George Washington, George Washington, George Washington, George Washington, and last but not least, George Washington. I know old George has been dead for two hundred years. But he sure looks good in green. Now, thanks to Bobby, my stack of dollar bills was gone.

Along with my clients.

See, I'm a detective. Mila and I solve

mysteries together. For a dollar a day, we make problems go away. We've had some pretty cool cases: missing bicycles, haunted scarecrows, marshmallow monsters.

But now all we had was free time.

Mila found me in my basement office. "What's Solofsky up to this time?" she grumbled.

"Stealing our clients," I said. I handed her a white index card. Mila read it out loud:

```
NEED A GHOST BUSTED?
Who Ya Gonna Call?
Bobby Solofsky!

For 99 cents a day, I make ghosts hit the road.

CALL 555-6976
```

"I wonder where he got that idea from," I muttered. I pulled out a copy of our business card.

NEED A MYSTERY SOLVED?
Call Jigsaw Jones
or Mila Yeh!
For a dollar a day,
we make problems go away
CALL 555–4523
or 555–4374

But that's Bobby Solofsky for you. He doesn't bother to think up his own ideas when he can steal somebody else's. The thing is, Solofsky couldn't even copy right. *I make ghosts hit the road?* It didn't even rhyme!

Mila tugged on her long black hair. "So Solofsky is in the ghost-busting business. What's that got to do with us?"

"Maybe nothing, maybe everything," I said. Sure, we were regular detectives. But sometimes our cases involved ghosts and goblins, too. Just that week, Lucy Hiller had claimed there was a ghost in her house.

She wanted to hire us to figure out what was going on. "Lucy heard that Solofsky got rid of some first grader's ghost. So she hired him to bust her ghost. And guess what? Poof!" I threw my hands up as if I'd just done a magic trick. "Solofsky solves the case . . . and now he's the number one ghost-buster in town."

Mila shook her head. "There's no such thing as ghosts," she said firmly. "I smell a rat."

"Yeah," I agreed. "A rat that smells like Bobby Solofsky . . . on gym day."

Now, I'm a simple guy. I believe in clues and cold hard facts. And I knew for a fact that Solofsky was up to something. It was time to take some air out of his balloon.

Chapter Two

Bad for Business

Before school the next day, everybody was buzzing about Solofsky's new ghost-busting business. *Buzz, buzz, buzz.* I felt like I was inside a beehive. And I kept getting stung.

"I heard he got rid of Lucy's ghost!" Athena Lorenzo gushed. "Even *Jigsaw* couldn't solve that case."

"That's because Jigsaw's a detective, not a ghost-buster," Mike Radcliff said. "He's okay with regular cases. But Bobby's an

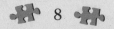

expert on anything that involves, um, really weird stuff."

I sat in my seat, fuming in silence.

"Don't let it bother you, Jigsaw," Mila whispered to me. "It's just one case. We'll get more."

All I wanted to do was forget about ghosts for a while. But that wasn't going to happen.

It was the week before Halloween. Things in Room 201 were a little spookier than usual. For our math lesson, we added and subtracted witches. For language arts, we practiced writing sentences about mummies and monsters. At circle time, our teacher, Ms. Gleason, read us a ghost story. And as a special treat, we got to play Candy Corn Bingo and Tic-Tac-Boo.

I guess you could say that by lunchtime, I had ghosts on the brain and bats in the belfry. We lined up to go to the

cafeteria. Bobby stood in front of me. I tried to ignore him.

It was like trying to ignore an 800-pound gorilla. Yeesh.

"Looks like I finally got you beat, Theodore," Solofsky said. "No one's going to hire you anymore. Not when there's a real ghost-buster in town."

I stared straight ahead. *Hum-dee-dum, dee-dum-dum*.

"You know the problem with you, Jones?" Solofsky continued. "You're old-fashioned. All the private detective stuff is, like, ancient history."

"Is that right?" I said.

Solofsky burped, then nodded. "Me? I'm all about the future. Ghosts, zombies, witches, and creeps — that's where the big money is."

"Uh-huh," I said.

"You'll be out of business by the end of the month," Solofsky predicted.

 11

"I'm shaking in my boots," I muttered.

Solofsky looked down at my sneakers. "You're not wearing boots," he said. He's about as quick as a three-legged turtle.

I sighed. "What do you *really* want, Solofsky?"

"I just wanted to see the look on your face when I told you I got three new clients today," Solofsky boasted. "How many did you get?"

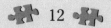

I didn't exactly need a calculator. The answer was a big fat zero. Still, I replied, "That's my business, Solofsky, not yours."

Solofsky just laughed. "Face it, Theodore. You're all washed up." He laughed extra loudly, like he was putting on a big show for everyone to watch.

There was no point in arguing with a guy like that. I needed time to think, and watching Solofsky hop around like a hyena with hiccups wasn't helping. I had a bunch of questions knocking around in my head like pinballs.

How come there were suddenly so many ghosts in town?

Why did everyone think Bobby could get rid of them?

Then there was the biggest question of all. Could Solofsky be right?

Maybe I *was* washed up, after all.

I was a detective with no clients.

I felt like a hamburger without a bun.

Chapter Three

Invisible

Over lunch, Mila and I shared our troubles — and our potato chips.

"Ralphie Jordan hired Solofsky to bust his ghost," Mila told me, chomping on a chip. "Kim Lewis and Eddie Becker, too." She started adding up ghosts on her fingers. "Then there's Lucy's ghost, and the other one you already told me about."

"Arnie Ellison," I reminded her. "He's a first grader. A new kid in town. He was Solofsky's first client."

"That's five ghosts this week," Mila said.

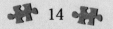

"I find that hard to believe. There's something fishy going on here."

"It doesn't take a detective to solve that mystery," I said, taking a long sip from my juice box. "Solofsky is behind it. But we need proof."

"Hmmm," Mila said.

"Is that a good 'hmmm' or a bad 'hmmm'?" I asked.

Mila shrugged. "It's a 'wait and see'

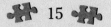

hmmm," she replied. "We don't know enough yet. We have to figure out a plan."

"You're right," I agreed. "And I know just where to start."

My dad always says that every businessman relies on his reputation. If people think you're an expert on aardvarks, they will come to you with their aardvark problems. If people think Solofsky is an expert ghost-buster, they will go to him with their ghost problems.

I pulled out my journal. I scribbled a page full of notes. Mostly it was a long list of questions — questions without answers.

Mila and I decided to start by talking to Arnie Ellison. There was just one problem. We had no idea who he was. And we weren't the only ones.

"Arnie Ellison? That kid with the ghost?" Helen

Zuckerman wrinkled her nose. "I don't know what he looks like. Maybe he's invisible. Ha, ha!" Helen clapped me on the back. Hard. "Get it? Invisible! Like a ghost!"

I got it, all right. Helen Zuckerman wanted to be the class clown. Too bad she was about as funny as homework.

"I think he's kind of short," Stringbean Noonan told us. "And, um, he definitely has . . . hair."

"Very helpful, Stringbean," Mila said, rolling her eyes. "That rules out all the first-grade boys who are bald!"

"Arnie gave me a cookie once," Joey Pignattano recalled fondly. His face glowed at the

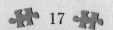

memory. "It was a great cookie. Chocolate chip with caramel clusters. Moist, but not *too* chewy."

"What about Arnie?" I reminded him. "What did he look like?"

"Oh." Joey shrugged. "I don't remember. But if you see him, can you find out if he has any more of those cookies?"

I sighed. We were getting nowhere. Everyone had heard of Arnie Ellison. And everyone had talked to him at least once or twice. But not a single person in our class could remember what he looked like. Maybe Helen was right. Maybe Arnie *was* invisible.

Mila and I finally tracked him down with the help of my neighbor Wingnut O'Brien. He directed us to a long table in the cafeteria. Everyone was clustered around one end of it, staring at a skinny boy with eyes like a lizard.

"The lights started flickering," the boy

said. "And then all the dishes flew through the air and slammed into the wall! *Crash! Blam! Bang!*"

"Then what happened?" one of the girls asked, her eyes shining with excitement.

"Then Bobby pulled out his ghost-busting equipment and we zapped the ghost together," the boy said proudly. "It won't be bothering me anymore."

Mila and I looked at each other in disbelief. We were both thinking the same thing. We'd found our invisible man. And thanks to his ghost, he wasn't so invisible anymore.

"Excuse me," I said politely. "My name is Jigsaw Jones. This is Mila Yeh. Do you mind if we ask you a few questions?"

Arnie folded his hands behind his head. He leaned back and grinned. "Ask away!"

Before I could speak, I felt a hand squeeze my shoulder. "Why are you bothering my client, Theodore?" Bobby Solofsky's voice scraped against my ears like chalk on a blackboard.

He was really getting on my nerves.

"It's okay, Bobby," Arnie quickly said. When I saw the look on his face, I almost hurled. Arnie's eyes were shining. His cheeks were glowing. He was smiling up at Solofsky like he was a hero.

Go figure.

"Stay away from my clients," Bobby growled. "If you've got questions about my business, just ask me. Or better yet, I'm busting Kim's ghost after school today. Come along and watch. Unless you're too chicken."

"We'll be there," I said gladly. It sounded too good to be true. We would watch Solofsky do his ghost-buster routine, and then we would bust *him*!

Chapter Four

Hiding Out

It was a dark and stormy night. Okay, it was only the afternoon, but it was raining pretty hard. I waited for Mila outside Kim Lewis's house at four o'clock sharp. Mila was singing as she came up the block:

"The itsy-bitsy ghost climbed up onto the roof.
Down came the rain and made the ghost go POOF!
Out came the sun and dried up all the rain.

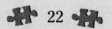

*And the itsy-bitsy ghost went . . .
OOMPHFF!"*

That last part wasn't in the song. It was
the sound Mila made when she tripped
over a tree root and fell.

"You okay?" I asked.

Mila looked at her scraped hands. "Sure,"
she said. "I didn't need that skin, anyway."

We huddled together under my sister's
pink umbrella (don't ask). I knocked on the
door. No answer. There was a sharp crack
of thunder. I knocked harder. The wind
suddenly picked up and raced through the
trees. The sky turned darker and darker. I
guess the sun was hiding out somewhere
warm and dry. I wished I could follow it.

Another crash of thunder echoed in
our ears. Lightning sliced through the
distant sky.

"I really don't feel like getting electrocuted
today," I said. We knocked even harder.

"BOO!" Solofsky shouted, suddenly flinging the door open.

Mila and I leaped back, right into a giant puddle. I winced as cold water sloshed into my shoes. Soggy socks — terrific.

"HA-HA-HA!" Bobby roared with laughter. "Scared you, didn't I? You've got to stay on your toes if you want to be a ghost-buster."

"Just let us in," I grumbled. "I'm as wet as a whale."

"Yeah, you smell a little fishy, too." Solofsky sniffed loudly.

"Har-har," Mila muttered, pushing her way inside.

Kim was sitting under the dining room table, holding tight to one of the legs. Her perfect white, tidy teeth were chattering. *Ratta-tatta, ratta-tatta.* She was either cold or terrified. If I was a betting man, I would have put my money on "terrified."

Mila and I wiped our feet on the mat. I stuck my sister's lousy pink umbrella by the door (I told you not to ask). "What's wrong, Kim?" Mila wondered. "You look like you've seen a —"

"Ghost?" Solofsky interrupted.

Kim didn't answer right away. She just waved us over. When we got close enough, she whispered, "The ghost always comes around this time." Her eyes darted back and forth. "My big sister, Kayla, is upstairs doing homework. She won't be able to help. Kayla doesn't know anything about ghosts."

"That's where I come in," Bobby said proudly. He placed a large cardboard box on the dining room table with a thud. "Never fear, Solofsky is here."

Oh, brother.

Suddenly, Mila squeezed my arm.

Ohhhhhhhhhhhhh . . .

I heard it, too. A low, shivering moan.

It was a creepy noise, echoing through

the room. The hairs on the back of my neck snapped to attention like soldiers. "Kim, is your sister playing a trick on us?" Mila whispered.

Kim shook her head.

Bwwwwwaaaaaaaaa . . .

"Is there anybody else home?" I asked.

Kim shook her head and squeezed her eyes shut. If Kim was faking it, she was doing a great job.

The moans and groans faded in and

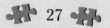

out. "It sounds like it's in the next room," Kim said, pointing down a darkened hallway. There was a sudden, loud crash. And then everything was quiet. Dead quiet.

Suddenly, the lights flickered and died. We were alone in the dark. We edged closer together under the table. "Maybe you should investigate," Kim suggested.

"Hey," I retorted, "you hired Solofsky, remember? Let him take care of it."

It was hard to stay still. Every detective instinct told me to get up and snoop around. But this was Solofsky's case. I wanted to see how he would handle it.

And, okay, it's not like I was *dying* to wrestle a ghost. Not unless I was getting paid for it — and I wasn't. So I didn't.

Instead I peered into the darkness. The lights were off, and the sky was overcast, but I could still see a little bit. I thought I saw something in the shadows. It crept past the window and slunk into a corner.

"Kim," I asked. "Do you have a cat?"

"No," she said.

"A dog?"

"No."

"How about a small water buffalo?" I asked hopefully.

"What?!"

"Don't mind Jigsaw," Mila quickly told Kim. "He's a great detective, but he's got a weird sense of humor."

"I think there's something moving out there," I explained.

"GET AWAY, GHOST!!" Solofsky suddenly roared. He pulled something out of his cardboard box. It looked like a water gun. "I SAID, 'GET OUT!'" he cried.

The lights flickered again. When they flickered on, the groans returned. When the power went out, the groaning seemed to stop. A few feet from us, Solofsky was putting on a first-rate show.

He threw down the water gun. He reached

into the box again and grabbed what looked like a Dust Buster. It had a flashing light on top, with pipe cleaners and rubber hoses taped to the sides. Solofsky flipped a switch and the whirring sound of a vacuum filled the room. "You heard me, ghost!" he shouted. "HIT THE ROAD!"

And just like that, it stopped.

The lights came back on.

The moans faded, then fell silent.

Solofsky gave me a triumphant grin, like a cat that swallowed a parakeet. "All safe now," he told Kim. He held out his empty palm. "That'll be ninety-nine cents, tax included."

Chapter Five

A Nutty Story

The next day, Mila and I had to take care of some unfinished business.

We found Arnie Ellison on the playground at recess. He was hanging on the monkey bars, surrounded by a group of first graders. I guess they just couldn't get enough of his ghost stories. But when Arnie saw us, he sent them away. "I've got important things to do," he told them proudly. "Jigsaw Jones wants to talk to me."

I eyed him closely. It was strange, but I could see why everyone had such a tough

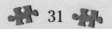

time remembering Arnie Ellison. He was kind of forgettable, like he blended into the wallpaper. He had scruffy hair, small ears, a stuffy nose, and a shirt that was about two sizes too big for him. There was nothing all that unique about Arnie. Except for one thing: He had seen a ghost.

"I've heard all about you guys," Arnie said, pulling a half-eaten sandwich from his jacket pocket. He waved it toward us. "Want a bite? It's raspberry jelly, my favorite."

"No peanut butter?" I asked. What kind of kid eats jelly sandwiches without the peanut butter? That's nutty.

Arnie shook his head. "Peanut butter? Blech! For me, it's all jelly, all the time." He took an enormous bite of the sandwich, then swiped his arm across his mouth to wipe off the jelly.

"So what do you guys want?" Arnie asked us.

"Well —" I paused, slightly annoyed. "We'll ask the questions, raspberry-breath. "

Mila chimed in, smiling warmly. "We just wanted to hear about your adventures with the ghost," she explained.

Arnie grinned. "Well, I try not to brag," he said.

I groaned softly, but Mila jabbed me in the ribs with her elbow. Ouch. I guess I got the point. I shut my trap and listened.

"Oh, please?" Mila said, pleading. "We would love to learn how you defeated a real, live ghost!"

Arnie ate it up, believing every word. He nodded proudly. "Yeah, I saw a ghost. It was big and super scary!"

"Tell me all about it, every detail!" Mila exclaimed. "You must be so brave."

Arnie blushed. "Well, I guess I am pretty brave," he admitted.

"What exactly did the ghost do?" Mila asked. She looked at me and winked.

Arnie hesitated. "Um, well, you know, typical ghost stuff. Loud noises. Banging around. And, oh, yeah, there was a lot of groaning." I thought it sounded an awful lot like the ghost at Kim's house. But who knows, maybe the ghosts were brothers.

"The ghost came every day for a whole week," Arnie went on, shivering. "That's when Bobby used his super-duper ghost-zapper to scare it away!"

"What made you call Solofsky — er, I mean, Bobby — for help?" I interrupted. "Are you friends with him?"

"Oh, no," Arnie said quickly. "I moved to town at the beginning of the school year. We used to live near the ocean. It was awesome. But then my mom got a new job, so we moved here, and . . ." Arnie frowned, and his lower lip started to wobble. "I didn't know anyone. It was like I didn't even exist before."

"Before?" I repeated.

Arnie's grin was back. "Before my ghost! Now everyone knows who I am!"

"And how did Bobby end up helping you?" I prodded.

Arnie nibbled on his thumbnail. "I guess he was just being nice," he said. "Bobby would help anyone. Isn't he amazing?"

I had a violent coughing attack.

"Bobby is the nicest guy I ever met," Arnie continued, his eyes as bright as new pennies. "Don't you think?"

I looked up at the sky.

I looked down at my boots.

I glanced at Mila, who was trying not to laugh.

Then I looked back at Arnie. I could see it in his eyes. He really did like Solofsky. Go figure.

"Yeah," I mumbled. "He's really . . . uh . . . something else."

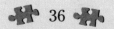

Chapter Six

When Marshmallows Attack

After recess, Mila and I trooped back to room 201. "Bobby's got to be faking the ghosts somehow," Mila whispered to me. "You remember how he fooled Sally Ann Simms with the floating egg trick."

"The Case of the Stinky Science Project," I recalled. "Don't remind me. Solofsky is always picking on somebody smaller than him."

Mila slid into her seat. "I don't know, Jigsaw," she said. "You heard Arnie. He thinks Solofsky is great. He doesn't feel cheated. He's happy! Maybe Solofsky really was trying to help."

"Yeah, and boa constrictors just want a hug," I muttered.

Ms. Gleason stood in front of the class. She clapped softly, *clap, clap*. We responded by clapping back three times, *CLAP, CLAP, CLAP*. It was our signal to stop talking and start listening.

"Boys and girls," Ms. Gleason began. "Since Halloween is almost here —"

"Woo-hoo!" Ralphie Jordan cried, pumping his fist in the air. "Free candy!"

"Yes, Ralphie, the dentists in town are very excited about it, too," Ms. Gleason said with a smile. We all laughed. "I thought we'd spend this afternoon sharing some scary experiences. Maybe they could serve as 'story starters' for your writing journals."

Eddie Becker waved his hand in the air. "I've got a million scary stories," he boasted.

"Did you hear the one about the guy with the hook? See, these kids are out in the woods and —"

"Actually, Eddie, today I'd like us to focus on real-life scary stories," Ms. Gleason explained. "I want each of you to take out your journals and a pencil. Write about something scary that has happened to you. Don't worry about getting the words down perfectly. Let this be your sloppy copy. We can revise later on."

Soon all I could hear was the sound of pencils scratching on paper. Too bad my brain couldn't think of anything.

Ugh. Writer's block. What a rotten feeling.

Then it hit me like a ton of water balloons. I wrote:

Once I went camping in the woods. I thought a lake monster stole all the marshmallows. But it wasn't a monster.

It was my dad. I hit him with a rock. He wasn't a happy camper.

I added a picture:

"Time's up, class," Ms. Gleason said. "Who would like to share their story?"

Athena Lorenzo raised her hand. Ms. Gleason invited her to the front of the classroom. Athena told us about the time that the power went out in her house. She was stuck in the dark all night long.

That got me wondering about the ghost in Kim's house. Was it a power blackout?

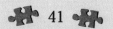

But that didn't explain the groaning. Hmmm.

Danika Starling read a story. When she was little, she got lost at the mall.

"Oh, goodness," Ms. Gleason said. "That must have been very frightening."

Danika looked at Ms. Gleason and nodded. "Very," she said.

Ralphie told us about a vampire who lives in his closet. "He's tall and green and every night he sneaks out to get me. *He vants to suck my blood!*" Ralphie finished, in a funny accent.

"Now, Ralphie, did that really happen?" Ms. Gleason asked. But you could tell she wasn't mad. Ralphie had that special gift. Everybody liked him.

Geetha Nair read her story. It was almost impossible to hear, because she's so shy. Geetha didn't look up at us once. Her story was about the first day of kindergarten.

"Aw, what's scary about that?" Solofsky complained.

Geetha's face flushed pink. "It was scary to me," she said softly.

"Everyone gets scared by different things," Ms. Gleason told the class. "Bobby, would you like to share your story?"

I leaned forward in my seat. Maybe Solofsky would make a mistake. Maybe he would accidentally admit that he wasn't busting real ghosts. I listened closely.

Bobby ran his tongue over his teeth, making a sucking noise. He scuffed his feet. "Nothing much scares me," he said, "except for spelling tests."

Everybody laughed.

Solofsky continued, "So this is a story about someone else getting scared. One time on vacation, there was this kid on the beach, and a sand crab crawled up his back. He was totally flipping out. But I

swiped the crab off him. I was a hero. The end."

Oh, brother. Gag me with a spoon. Bobby Solofsky, a hero? That was about as likely as me playing third base for the New York Mets.

Next up was Joey Pignattano. Joey's a good guy and a real friend, even if all he ever thinks about is food.

"Until yesterday," Joey began, "the

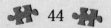

scariest thing that ever happened to me was when I went to get myself a mini-doughnut. You know, the kind with powdered sugar and some chocolate sprinkles on top? When I got to the kitchen, I discovered the box was empty!"

See what I mean about Joey and food? It's the only thing on his mind.

"But yesterday, something even scarier happened," Joey said in a hushed voice.

"What? You lost a Twinkie?" I joked.

Joey shook his head. "Nah, but it was almost *that* bad."

We held our breath, wondering what could scare Joey more than a lost Twinkie. *Two* lost Twinkies?

"Yesterday," he said, "I found out that my house was haunted . . . by a ghost!"

Chapter Seven
A Warning

I cornered Joey near the cubbies at the end of the school day. "Let me take your case," I said.

"What case?" Joey asked, pulling two Oreos out of his backpack. He ate the top off of one cookie, then the other. He gave each layer of frosting a good, long lick. Then he crammed the two cookies together. "Double-stuffed!" he exclaimed. "What case?" he asked again. The trouble was, he'd just crammed a double-stuffed cookie into his mouth. It sounded more like "Whuf aif?"

"The Case of the Groaning Ghost." I glanced over my shoulder to make sure no one could hear us. "I want to solve your mystery."

"But there is no mystery, Jigsaw," Joey answered. "It's just a ghost. Bobby said he'd get rid of it. Just ninety-nine cents. That's cheaper than you," he pointed out.

"Big whoop, a penny," I said.

"Jigsaw," Joey said, "you are a great detective. Everybody knows that. But ghosts are Bobby's specialty."

I frowned. I thought about it. And then I said something I wasn't eager to say. "I'll do it for free," I told Joey.

"For free?" he asked, chomping down on another Oreo. "I don't know. Bobby is an expert. What do you know about ghosts?"

"Let's make a deal," I offered. "For a cookie a day, I'll make your ghost go away."

"You want me to pay you in cookies?" Joey yelped. He was outraged. "NEVER!"

"No, no, no. You got it backwards, Joey. I will pay YOU in cookies," I corrected him. "One cookie for every day it takes me to solve your case."

Joey grinned, his teeth black with crumbs. "It's a deal!"

I pulled out my detective notebook and turned to a new page. It was time to get started on this case!

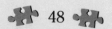

Case: The Groaning Ghost
Client: Joey Pignattano
Suspects: BOBBY SOLOFSKY!

I had to let Mila know that we had a new case. I wrote her a secret note. I used a push back code.

3ZH 1IBWF5F 3QHZ 5HFXJ

In each word, I "pushed" all the letters forward by a certain number. Then I stuck that number in front of each word. To solve the code, Mila just had to push back each letter by the right number.

For example, 3ZH meant that "Z" got pushed back three letters to "W," and "H" got pushed back to "E." So the word spelled "WE."

5HFXJ was code for "CASE." It was easy, once you knew the trick.

Mila had figured out the code by the time

we stood outside, waiting in line for the bus. When I spotted her, she slid her finger across her nose. That was our secret sign. When you're a detective, you've got to watch what you say. The ears have walls . . . or something like that.

"I'm glad Joey hired us to take his case," Mila said. "I could use the money."

I would tell her about the cookie bargain another day. Right now, we had important

work to do. "Joey says the ghost showed up yesterday after school," I informed her. "We should scope out his house today."

"Hunting for ghosts, Theodore?" a voice suddenly said. Bobby Solofsky had crept up behind us. The dirty sneak.

I spun around. "We're talking about a case, Solofsky," I said. "Nothing that would interest you."

Bobby shook his head slowly, tapping his finger against his lips. "You'd better be careful, Theodore. You don't know what you're messing with."

I scowled at Solofsky. "What's that supposed to mean?"

"You forgot two things," Solofsky warned. "First: Ghosts are a dangerous business."

I shrugged. "Yeah, sure. What's the second thing?"

Solofsky glared at me. "Second: Ghosts are *my* business. Stay out of my way."

Chapter Eight
A Hungry Ghost?

"I'm glad you're here," Joey said as we stepped into his house. He offered us a plate of jelly doughnuts, but I waved them away. Sometimes it's best not to mix business with sugar. "This is around the same time the ghost showed up yesterday. Did you bring your ghost-zappers?" Joey asked.

Mila snapped her fingers. "Darn, I left my ghost-zapper at home! It's right next to my vampire stake and my werewolf muzzle!"

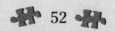

Joey glanced at Mila with newfound respect.

He brought us into his living room and explained, "Bobby said he could sense that my ghost liked to follow a set pattern."

"Solofsky was here?" I immediately asked. "When?"

"He just left," Joey admitted. He paused to lick some jelly off his fingers. "Bobby came by with a bunch of ghost-busting stuff, but I told him this was your case now."

"Thanks," I said.

"No problem, Jigsaw," Joey answered. He held out his hand. "Did you bring the cookie?"

Mila looked at me in surprise. "What?"

"I'll explain later," I muttered, handing Joey two chocolate-chip cookies for good measure.

Just as I gave Joey his payment, a low moaning swept through the room.

"It's here!" Joey cried. "THE GHOST!"

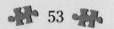 53

Oooooooooooooooh . . .

Ahhhhhhhhhhhhhhh . . .

We froze in our tracks. Mila gestured down the hall. "What's down there?" she whispered to Joey.

"The kitchen," he answered.

Bwwwwwaaaaaaaaa . . .

"It's in there," Mila decided. "Let's go, Jigsaw."

She tiptoed toward the ghostly groans.

"Right behind you," I said, grateful that

she was there. Mila was my partner. Where she went, I went.

We took one step down the hall. Then another. The groaning got louder and louder.

AHHHHHHHHHHHH . . .

OHHHHHHHHHHHH . . .

"Hello?" Mila said softly.

And just like that, the noise stopped.

Everything went quiet.

"Do you think it's gone?" I whispered.

"I hope so," Mila replied.

"Hey," I said, looking around. "Where's Joey?"

CRASH!

Mila and I jumped. The noise came from the kitchen. The ghost was back!

We heard footsteps. They clomped toward us, closer and closer. My heart pounded like a bass drum.

"Oh, rats! I knocked over the cookie jar." It was Joey. He'd gone into the kitchen

through the archway on the other side. I guess once he started walking to the kitchen, nothing could stop him.

"Anybody want a dirty cookie?" Joey offered.

"Don't touch anything," I told him. "We have to search the scene of the crime."

"Yeah," Mila said, grinning. "Try not to eat any clues."

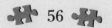

I began by standing at the entranceway, looking things over. Besides a dozen cookies and shattered pottery on the floor, nothing seemed out of place. I scanned the counter: cookbooks, blender, toaster, walkie-talkie, telephone. I shivered.

"Scared?" Joey asked.

"No," I replied. "Just cold."

I pulled out my magnifying glass.

 57

"What are you looking for?" Joey wondered.

"I don't know," I answered. Just then, I spotted something. "Hellllllooo. What's this?"

There was sticky red goo on the light switch. I examined it under the magnifying glass. Yes, it was sticky red goo all right. I smelled it. I dabbed it with my finger. And then I tasted it.

"Jigsaw!" Mila cried. "Gross me out the door!"

"It's a clue," I said triumphantly. "Jelly on the light switch."

"Joey was eating jelly doughnuts when we got here," Mila said.

I sighed. So maybe it wasn't much of a clue after all.

"Strange," Mila said, turning to the counter. She picked up the walkie-talkie. "The red light is on." She turned a little dial and it flicked off. "Where's the other one?" She asked Joey.

He shrugged. "Beats me. That's not even mine," he said. "Maybe Bobby left it here. He had a lot of ghost-busting equipment, like I told you before."

"Why would Solofsky need a walkie-talkie?" I asked.

Mila crossed her arms, puzzled. "It could be for eavesdropping," she guessed. "If he's listening in on the other walkie-talkie, he could hear if something is going on."

"Maybe," I answered. "Or maybe . . ."

"What?" Mila asked.

I glanced at Joey. "Never mind," I said to Mila. "It's probably nothing."

Mila shivered. "Joey, why do you have the window open? It's miserable outside."

"I don't know," Joey said. He snapped it closed. "I didn't open it."

"Hmmm," Mila said. I didn't have to ask her what kind of "hmmm" it was. I knew exactly what she was thinking. The pieces were coming together. Someone — or something — had come through that open window.

But who?

"Why isn't the floor wet?" Mila wondered. "If someone came through the window, shouldn't there be footprints?"

"Good question," I said.

"Maybe," Joey suggested, "ghosts don't have feet."

Chapter Nine

The Stakeout

The next day at school, I overheard Bobby Solofsky talking with Mike Radcliff. They were making plans for after school — plans that didn't include riding the bus home. I decided to keep an eye on them.

"Be careful," Mila warned me when I told her about it.

"Sure thing, partner," I answered. "I'll be as careful as a bullfrog hugging a porcupine."

Mila rolled her eyes.

The minute the school bell sounded, I

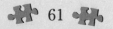

darted outside. I hid behind a bush. And waited. And watched. That's the detective business in a nutshell. It's not all excitement and glory. A lot of it is just putting one foot in front of the other, following the clues. Hey, it's a living.

Bobby Solofsky and Mike Radcliff pushed past the school doors and headed in my direction. Solofsky was horsing around, and Radcliff was snorting and laughing. When they took off down the street, I tailed them.

Fortunately, I was in disguise. If they spotted me, they wouldn't know who I was. I was wearing a long trenchcoat and a big, wide hat and sunglasses. I made sure to keep my distance, ducking behind trees and parked cars whenever possible.

They were going into town. *Maybe they need supplies*, I thought. *Ghost supplies.*

First Solofsky and Radcliff stopped at Barney Black's Sweetshop. My stomach

rumbled, but I cooled my heels outside. More watching, more waiting.

Next I followed them to Cosmic Comics. I peeked at them through the window. They both walked to the back of the store and pulled out a stack of comic books. Then they sat down on the floor and read.

Oh, brother. I walked across the street and leaned against a wall. I pulled out my superspy newspaper. It had two eyeholes cut in the front, so I could hide behind it but still watch the action. Not that there was any action to watch.

The seconds ticked by. The minutes piled up like dirty laundry. Time crawled along like a chubby caterpillar. And still, nothing happened.

Like I said, that's detective work. The tough cases are like walnuts; they don't crack that easily. So you watch and you wait and maybe, if you get really bored, you think.

So that's what I did. I thought about the case. I was still confused by yesterday's visit to Joey's house. The pieces didn't seem to fit.

The kitchen window was open, but there were no footprints. There was a jelly stain on the light switch, but Joey had just been eating a jelly doughnut. There was a walkie-talkie in the kitchen, but no proof that it was used.

My feet hurt, my eyes itched, and my

brain felt like pea soup. Finally, Solofsky and Radcliff left the comic book store. I followed them home. And that was that. A fastball down the middle, and a swing and a miss. Some days are like that.

I made it home just in time for dinner.

"What's up, Worm?" my brother Nick asked. "You seem kind of grouchy."

"Nothing is up," I grumbled. "And don't call me Worm."

"Whatever you say, *Shorty*," Daniel chimed in.

Big brothers, yeesh. You can count on them to kick you when you're down. And then give you a noogie.

"Is something wrong?" my mom asked.

I pushed my broccoli around on the plate. "I'm working on a case," I said, sighing. "It's not going real well."

"No suspects?" my dad asked.

"One suspect," I replied. "And I know he did it. But I can't prove it."

 65

"If you don't have proof, then how do you know?" my dad asked.

"You wouldn't understand," I said.

Dad wrinkled his forehead. "I thought you used to say that mysteries are like jigsaw puzzles."

I nodded. "Yeah, you have to solve them one piece at a time."

"Well," my dad said, "it seems to me like you're jumping to conclusions before you put all the pieces into place."

Grams seemed like she had something to add. She looked at us . . . and burped. "Whoopsies," she said, her eyes twinkling with delight.

"GRAMS!" my sister, Hillary, squealed.

My brothers laughed hysterically. Even my mom and dad thought it was funny. Hey, it *was* funny. Grandmothers burping — that's comedy! Hillary laughed so hard that milk squirted out of her nose.

Don't ask why, but I felt better after that.

And maybe my dad had a point. Maybe I was so sure that Solofsky was the groaning ghost that I had missed something along the way. Could it be possible?

The phone rang, and my brother Billy jumped up to get it. "Yo," he said into the receiver. Then he frowned. "It's for you, Sherlock. Make it snappy. I've got a hot date tonight."

"Really? Is the circus in town?" Hillary scoffed.

I took the call in the dining room. It was Joey.

"The ghost came back this afternoon!" Joey told me. "But this time, it stole one of my cookies! This means war!"

"For real?" I asked.

"You have to solve this case," he pleaded. "A ghost is one thing. But a cookie thief is a huge problem!"

"Slow down," I urged him. "Are you sure?"

"Sure, I'm sure!" Joey exclaimed. "When

it comes to food, I'm always sure. That ghost stole a marshmallow cookie this time!"

Joey would never lie. Then it hit me. I had been spying on Solofsky all afternoon. He hadn't been anywhere near Joey's house. He was innocent.

My jaw might have hit the floor in surprise. If Solofsky wasn't haunting Joey, then who was? Unless . . .

What if there really was a ghost?

Chapter Ten
Secrets and Lies

We had to start at the beginning. It was like when you do those mazes in an activity book. Once you run into a dead end, you have to backtrack. Try to figure out where you made the wrong turn.

Mila and I started with Arnie Ellison.

"Come on in," he greeted us the next afternoon, opening his front door. We'd asked him at school

if we could drop by. Arnie led us upstairs to his bedroom. This whole thing began with Arnie. Somehow, we must have missed something. "I love visitors!" Arnie said, bouncing onto his bed. "Back where I used to live, I had lots of friends. But now . . ." He looked away.

I eyeballed the room. The walls were mostly covered with pictures of Arnie and his friends. Strangely, there were a few blank spots, as if some photos had been taken down. Maybe they had gotten into a fight, I guessed. "What used to be there?" I asked, pointing to one of the blank spots.

"There? Oh, gee, nothing," Arnie said. His nose twitched. His eyes darted up, down, all around. I instantly knew that he was lying. But why? Before I could ask more questions, an angry teenager barged in.

Think of a charging rhino, but without the charm. Yeesh.

"I told you to stay out of my stuff, Arnold!"

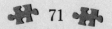 71

the teenager yelled. This, I gathered, was Arnie's big brother. Lucky Arnie.

"I never touched your stuff, Harry!" Arnie cried. "I promise." But I saw that his nose twitched again. He wasn't a great liar.

"Oh, yeah? This is the second time this week something's been taken from my room," Harry said.

Arnie suddenly noticed the clock. "Oh, no," he cried. "I'm late!" He leaped off the bed and headed for the door.

"I'll get your stuff back, Harry," he promised. "But I gotta go." And then, he was gone.

Arnie just disappeared. Like a ghost.

Harry sank down on the bed. He didn't look mad anymore, just confused. "I don't know what's going on with that kid," he said with a sigh.

"Do you know where he's going?" Mila asked.

Harry shook his head. "No clue. He's

been running off every afternoon for a couple weeks." Harry shrugged. "You little kids are pretty weird."

Yeah, right, I thought. He should take a good look in the mirror. Teenagers aren't exactly a picnic in the park on a warm summer day.

"Can I ask you a question?" I said.

"You just did," Harry pointed out. Then he snickered, pleased with his cleverness.

Like I said: Teenagers. Yeesh.

"What did Arnie take from you?" I asked.

"My walkie-talkies," Harry answered.

Mila shot me a look. I nodded. We were both wondering the same thing. *How did that same walkie-talkie end up in Bobby's ghost-busting box?*

"He used to be good about staying out of my stuff," Harry confided. "But lately . . . It's that Solofsky kid, I just know it."

My ears perked up. "Who?"

"Arnie's a good kid," Harry said, ignoring my question. "But every summer, that weird Solofsky kid and his family rent a house on the beach for two weeks. Right in our old town. And every summer, he gets Arnie into trouble. This fall, we moved here — the same town where Solofsky lives. Now I have to deal with that kid all year." He rubbed his eyes, as if he had a headache.

"I know how you feel," I sympathized.

Chapter Eleven
Busting a Ghost

"Now we know that Bobby and Arnie are friends," Mila said as we walked home from Arnie's house.

"Yes, the pieces are coming together," I replied. "But why didn't he want us to know?" I thought of the missing pictures on Arnie's wall. I would have bet ten bucks that they were photos of Bobby Solofsky.

Mila stopped in her tracks. She grabbed me by the shoulders. "It's a two-man con," she explained. "They're working together."

"Like a team," I muttered.

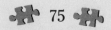

"Yes!" Mila cried. "One pretends to be a ghost . . ."

". . . and the other scares the ghost away!" I concluded. "It's brilliant — in a rotten kind of way. And that's why they need the walkie-talkies. That's how they created the groaning and the moaning!"

"Arnie didn't get tricked by Solofsky," Mila said. "It was Arnie who fooled *us*. And Solofsky helped him do it!"

"Come on," I said, tugging Mila's arm. "Let's end this once and for all."

When we got to Solofsky's house, I leaned on his doorbell until he opened the door.

"Whaddaya want, Theodore?" Solofsky grunted. "I'm busy."

"We need some help," I said. "We're having a little trouble with ghosts."

"Well, why didn't you say so?" he cooed

cheerfully. "I knew you'd come crawling to me for help sooner or later." He stepped aside and invited us in.

Solofsky threw himself down on the couch. He kicked his feet up on a table. Mila and I stood. "So what can I do for you?" Solofsky asked. He gave us a sour grin. "I usually charge ninety-nine cents a day. But for you? Let's make it two bucks a day."

He was feeling pretty good about himself, I noticed. Well, I was feeling pretty good, too. I was about to solve a case.

"We just need to ask you one question," Mila said.

"Oh?" Solofsky's eyes narrowed. Then he shrugged. "Why not? I'm the ghost expert. Ask anything you want."

"Was this ghost idea yours, or Arnie's?" I asked.

Solofsky bounced off the sofa like a Super Ball. "Arnie's got nothing to do with nothing," he protested.

 77

"Nothing to do with *anything*," Mila corrected him. "And actually, we think he has everything to do with it."

"We found the walkie-talkie at Joey's house," I told Solofsky. "The one that belongs to Arnie's brother. We figure that you opened the window, and Arnie climbed into the house that way."

"What about the flickering lights?" Solofsky asked.

"I'll admit, that part had me stumped," I said.

"But we found a jelly stain on the light switch," Mila added. "Arnie's favorite food."

"Then Arnie climbed back outside and groaned into his walkie-talkie," I continued. "But Arnie was smart. He probably cleaned up his wet footprints before he left."

Solofsky smiled. "I taught him that," he admitted.

"Arnie is your friend from summer vacation," I noted. Then I remembered

Solofsky's story from class. "And something tells me he's afraid of sand crabs."

Solofsky sank back against the couch. He tugged at his short, spiky hair. He pressed his lips together. He shook his head. Then he nodded. It was like he was having a fight with himself. Finally, he looked up at me.

"Okay, Jones, you got me," he confessed. "But you can't tell anyone."

"Oh?" I said. "You tricked half the kids in our class!"

"You've got to believe me," Solofsky pleaded. And for once, he didn't have that classic Solofsky sneer on his face. In fact, for the first time ever, he looked like he was sorry. "I didn't mean to hurt anybody. I was just trying to do the right thing."

"The right thing?" I echoed. "I find that hard to believe."

Solofsky looked me right in the eye. "It's true."

I glanced at Mila, uncertain. "Okay, maybe

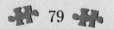

there's a first time for everything. You expect a medal?"

"Do you want to hear about it or not?" Solofsky asked.

"Just forget it, Solofsky." I turned to Mila. "Let's go."

"No, wait," Mila said. "Let's hear what Bobby has to say." She sat down on the couch. And after a minute, so did I.

Solofsky sighed. "I know Arnie from way back," he admitted. "Every summer, my family spends a few weeks at the beach. Arnie used to live there year-round. It was a sweet setup. We used to hang out together. He was a year younger than me, but I figured nobody would ever know about it. So we played together. You know, busted up sand castles, splashed people. Typical stuff you do at the beach."

"Go on," Mila said.

"When Arnie moved here, he didn't have

any friends," Solofsky said. He looked at the carpet. "But, well . . ."

"You didn't want everyone to know you were friends with a first grader," Mila guessed. "Because you were too cool."

Bobby nodded unhappily. "I know it was dumb," he admitted. "I kind of felt bad about it after a while. Then Arnie made up that story about having a ghost in his house. He thought it would make the other kids notice him. But no one believed him. So he came to me for help."

"He needed a witness," I said. "A hotshot guy like you."

"Now Arnie is famous," Bobby explained. "I mean, he's finally happy. He's not the new kid anymore. He's the kid who survived a ghost in his house!"

We sat in silence for a few minutes. Mila was the first to speak. "That was a nice thing to do," she said. "But what about the other kids? What about their ghosts?"

"So? What about them?" Bobby asked.

"You tricked them out of their money," I pointed out. "They thought you were chasing a ghost. But really, Arnie's story gave you an idea — and a partner. You saw an easy way to make some money."

"It made them happy," Bobby argued. "Everyone loves ghosts. People stand in line and pay money to go into haunted houses. Why shouldn't I make a lousy dollar for giving them a real-life scare?"

"It's not honest, that's why," Mila said.

Bobby shook his head. "Yeah, I know. But it didn't hurt anybody. Arnie was having so much fun. If I tell the truth now, everyone will know that Arnie was faking it. He'll be lonely all over again."

"There's nothing we can do," I said. "We can't keep piling lies on top of lies."

"Maybe there is a solution," Mila said. A smile grew on her face. "I have an idea."

Chapter Twelve

A Monster Bash

I stuck my hand into the bowl of brains.

I pulled out a chunk of gooey slime.

Then I popped it in my mouth.

Not bad at all.

"These brains are delicious, Mila!" I joked.

"Thanks." Mila plucked another slimy chunk out of the bowl. "My stepmom made them out of Jell-O, gummy worms, and cold spaghetti."

They went really well with the chocolate

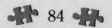

spiders, night crawlers, and vampire punch.

I looked around the room. Kim Lewis was bobbing for apples. Lucy Hiller was pinning the nose on the ugly green witch. Ralphie Jordan was painting a pumpkin. And Arnie Ellison, who used to have no friends in town, stood in the center of it all, with a huge grin on his face.

"Great party, Arnie!" Danika Starling told him, chomping on candy corn.

"Yeah, Arnie, this is awesome!" Joey agreed. Only it sounded more like, "Thish ish awefum!" Joey had two chocolate boo-cakes stuffed in his mouth.

Across the room, I saw something I never thought I'd see.

Bobby Solofsky lifted his chin in a nod. He smiled at me. I tried to smile back. But it's hard to teach an old dog new tricks.

"What's wrong, Jigsaw?" Mila asked.

 85

"Me," I answered. "I was wrong about Solofsky. I was so sure he was a trouble-maker that I missed important clues. We almost didn't solve the case."

"But we *did* solve it," Mila pointed out. "And now everyone's happy. Especially Arnie."

Bobby had agreed to Mila's plan. We used his ghost-busting money to throw a party, Arnie Ellison's Awesome Halloween Bash. We invited all the kids that Arnie "haunted." And Mila was right. Everybody was having a great time.

"I should have known better," I said. "I'm

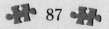

a detective. I'm supposed to follow the clues, one at a time. Instead, I made up my mind from the beginning." I shook my head. "I'll be right back, Mila. There's something I have to do."

It wasn't going to be much fun. But it had to be done. I walked across the room, over to Bobby Solofsky. I took a deep breath. Then I held out my hand. "I'm sorry, Solofsky."

"For what?" he asked in surprise.

"For making up my mind about you before I had all the facts," I told him. "I was wrong about you, Solofsky. You were trying to do the right thing. Well, sort of. In your own totally weird way."

Solofsky grinned.

"Thanks, Theodore — I mean, Jigsaw."

He held out his hand. And we shook on it.

Zap! Bzzzzzzzzz!

I yelped. A small shock sizzled through my arm.

"Bwaa-ha-ha!" Solofsky laughed. He opened his hand to reveal a joy buzzer. "Got you again, Theodore! Some things never change!"

I couldn't help it. I laughed, too. Because for once in his life, Bobby Solofsky was right.

Some things never do change.

About the Author

James Preller often draws upon his own life as a basis for his Jigsaw Jones books. Like Jigsaw, James Preller has a slobbering, sock-eating dog. Like Jigsaw, James was the youngest in a large family. His older brothers called him Worm and worse — yeesh! And so do Jigsaw's!

James and Jigsaw both love jigsaw puzzles, baseball, grape juice, and mysteries! But even though Jigsaw and James have so much in common, they are not the same person.

Unlike Jigsaw, James Preller is the author of many books for children. He lives in Delmar, New York, with his wife, Lisa, three kids — Nicholas, Gavin, and Maggie — his two cats, and his dog.

Learn more at www.jamespreller.com